Weekly Reader Children's Book Club presents

Who goes there, Lincoln?

About the Book

When Lincoln Farnum and his pals lost their clubhouse, Lincoln decided to use the old firehouse. Even though it was about to be torn down, the building would be a great place to hold a scary initiation for Hands and the Stickballers. The Plum Street Athletic Club had plenty of tricks to pull on their former rivals.

Mrs. Crauch said the firehouse was once an opera house and old Mrs. Patch called it "the end of the railroad." What it all meant Lincoln didn't know, but as usual, he got in plenty of trouble finding out!

The popular hero of *Who's in Charge Lincoln?*, *What's New, Lincoln?* and *What's the Prize, Lincoln?* is at it again scheming, dreaming, and having a mischievous good time.

Who

goes there, Lincoln?

by Dale Fife

Illustrated by Paul Galdone

COWARD, McCANN & GEOGHEGAN, INC.   *New York*

To My Friend, Jessie Hungerford

Who goes there, Lincoln?

1

IF CALICO HADN'T HAD KITTENS in Mrs. Crauch's bathtub, and if Pop hadn't read that article about the old firehouse, maybe Lincoln Farnum would never have learned about the ghost that haunted Plum Street.

It all started on Saturday morning over the pancakes. "Please pass the syrup," Lincoln said, attacking his third stack.

"You've had half a gallon already," Sissy said.

"No wonder he's so sticky," Sassy chimed in.

Lincoln ignored his twin sisters, took the bottle Mom handed him, and poured a golden lake around his buckwheat mountain.

Pop came out from behind the newspaper. "There's a story here about the old Plum Street firehouse. The city's going to tear it down."

9

Lincoln's older sister, Sara, who was dieting again, poured herself a cup of black coffee. "I thought Supervisor Williams was trying to save it."

The bearded supervisor lived at the other end of Plum Street.

"We can't save all old buildings," Pop said. "Now if it were historical. . . ."

"What makes a place historical?" Lincoln asked.

Pop stirred sugar into his coffee. "If something important happened there. History that influenced the future."

Mom spooned cereal into Baby Herman's mouth. "I wonder what the property will be used for."

"Maybe another carwash," Pop said.

"I'll fight that," Mom said.

In his highchair, Baby Herman picked up his bowl of cereal and poured it over his head.

Lincoln mopped him up. "What this street needs is a baby wash."

There was a knock on the door.

Lincoln answered.

Bunky Hanson, the kid from down the street, stood there.

"Special meeting of the Plum Street Athletic Club. Did you forget?"

How could he? Great things were happening to the club.

Lincoln took a last swallow of milk and shrugged into his jacket.

Outside, Wilbur, who lived across the hall, was waiting on the apartment steps. The three boys swaggered down Plum Street.

At the drugstore corner, Lincoln stopped and looked over at the old firehouse across the street. The big front doors and the windows had been boarded up for as long as he could remember. The old brick building was black with soot. Still, Lincoln thought, its cupola looked kind of homey. Maybe even historical.

Mrs. Patch, the very oldest person on Plum Street came by with her dog, Fats Butch. She stopped and looked across the street too.

"It's going to be torn down," Lincoln said.

"Ah, yes, the end of the railroad," Mrs. Patch said. Fats Butch pulled at his leash and she walked on.

"Railroad," Wilbur said. "I don't see any tracks."

"You know how she is," Lincoln said. "Come on, let's go."

2

THE BOYS TURNED THE CORNER and ambled along the side of Mr. Woods' drugstore. Their clubhouse was secret from almost everyone. Before they went through the gate in the high board fence behind the building, they looked around to see if anyone was watching. The coast was clear. Quickly they disappeared into the cement yard and made for a clump of bushes in the corner. Behind the shrubbery, secret steps led down to a hidden door. Lincoln pushed it open and they filed into the dim interior. Bunky threw the rusty bolt.

They sank into the three sagging chairs around the wobbly card table. The only light came through the small window near the ceiling which had once been the coal chute.

"It's sure neat having our own place," Wilbur said. He glanced around at the posters they had pasted over the grimy walls and the barred door to the rest of the cellar.

Lincoln banged on the table. One leg gave way. He righted it. "Meeting will come to order. Will the secretary get on with the minutes."

Wilbur kept them in his head. "We voted to ask Hands and his Stickballers to join our club."

Lincoln grinned. "We know how they jumped at the chance. I don't think they believed we had a real clubhouse until we told them they'd see it next Friday when we initiate them."

Big, cocky Hank Jacks lived on the other end of Plum Street. He was called "Hands" because his mitts were so big. Hands and his Stickballers were great athletes. With them in the club, the Plum Streeters would be champs in all sports.

"Well, how about the initiation?" Bunky asked.

"It's got to be something spectacular," Lincoln said. "Any ideas?"

"How about having them roll peanuts with their nose?"

"In here?" Wilbur asked. "There's no room."

"Call that spectacular?" Lincoln asked.

"Well, what's your idea?" asked Bunky.

Lincoln shrugged. "I can't think of anything spectacular either. We've got only a week. Say, Bunky, you were supposed to tell Mr. Woods about our new members."

"I did," Bunky said.

Stringy Mr. Woods had been allowing them to use the old coal cellar for a clubhouse for some time now.

"Then it's all set," Lincoln said.

There was a banging on the door. "LINCOLN! Open up. This very minute."

"It's Sassy," Lincoln said. He got up and opened the door a crack. "State your business."

"Mrs. Crauch's got an emergency. Mom said you'd go."

An emergency with Mrs. Crauch meant she needed an electric light bulb put in somewhere she couldn't reach, or maybe she wanted something heavy from the grocery store.

"Okay," he said.

Sassy poked her head around the door. "What a dump," she said.

"Meeting adjourned," Lincoln said, and the three of them headed for the outside.

When they got to the front of the drugstore, Mr. Woods was standing in the doorway. "Been wanting to talk to you boys," he said.

They sauntered over.

"I've been thinking over your plan of inviting the Stick-ballers to join up with you. The coal cellar is too small for so many. Besides, I need the space for storage. I'll have to ask you boys to move out right away."

"There isn't any other place for us to go," Lincoln said.

"Sorry about that," Mr. Woods said and hurried back into his drugstore.

The boys stood there, stunned.

Lincoln started toward Mrs. Crauch's.

Wilbur and Bunky followed along.

Finally, Bunky said: "It was dinky."

His voice sounded funny.

"Yeah," Wilbur said. "It was awfully dark inside and it had a funny smell."

Bunky kicked at a tin can. "Sassy said it was a dump."

"But it was *our* place," Lincoln said.

They had reached Mrs. Crauch's apartment. They huddled on the stoop.

Lincoln felt terrible, but Bunky and Wilbur looked so sad he felt sorry for them. "I'll think of something," he said, ringing the doorbell.

Their faces brightened.

"You always do," Bunky said.

Wilbur slapped him across the back. "Lunky Link."

Now what, Lincoln wondered, had made him open his big mouth. There was absolutely no place around Plum Street that he could get for a clubhouse.

3

"THANK GOODNESS, you've come," Mrs. Crauch fluttered as she opened the door and the boys filed into the crowded sitting room. Her apartment was very old, the oldest on Plum Street.

"What's the trouble?" Lincoln asked.

"Calico had kittens. Something must be done at once."

"Gee," Lincoln said. "I don't know anyone wants a cat."

"I don't intend to give them away—yet," Mrs. Crauch said, leading the way down the hall. "I just want them out of my bathtub."

Mrs. Crauch's bathtub was in the kitchen against the wall. It stood on four claws. A hinged, wooden top covered most of it.

The boys crowded around. There, on a towel, sat Calico, meowing, her kittens skittering about on the slippery tub.

Lincoln reached down to pet one of them. Calico complained.

"She's not used to company," Mrs. Crauch said. "Now if you boys will go into the bedroom and pull out that old trunk from the clothes closet, I'll empty it and make a bed in it for Calico and her family. Then she'll feel better, and I can take a bath again."

The three of them took turns pulling the heavy black trunk from the narrow closet.

"It's been here ever since my grandfather's time," Mrs. Crauch said, prying up the lid.

A strong odor of mothballs made Lincoln sneeze three times.

Mrs. Crauch started handing out what looked to Lincoln like very strange clothes. "You can take them to the junkman around the corner," she said.

Bunky looked at the shabby pants and suspenders she handed him. "He pays two cents a pound for rags," he said.

Mrs. Crauch held up a long black cape.

"Who wore such things?" Lincoln asked, taking it from her.

"They belonged to an actor," Mrs. Crauch said.

"An actor?" Lincoln said. "Did an actor really live on Plum Street?"

Mrs. Crauch handed Wilbur a black frock coat and broad-brimmed black hat. "I'll have you know that Plum Street was something once upon a time—when my father was a boy. There even was an opera house."

"An opera house! On Plum Street! Where?" Lincoln asked.

"It's still here. But now it's the firehouse," Mrs. Crauch said, doling out the rest of the clothes.

"I didn't know the firehouse was that old," Lincoln said. "Does that make it historical?"

"No, just an old building," Mrs. Crauch said. "My, I'm pleased to get rid of all those old things. Now I'll be able to fix up a bed for Calico and her kittens." She led the way to the front door.

"What happened to the actor?" Lincoln asked from the stoop. "Why didn't he take his clothes with him?"

"He disappeared. During the second act of *Julius Caesar,* Father said, with a dozen policemen surrounding the opera house."

"Was he a murderer?" Bunky asked, owl-eyed.

"No, the police were there to check on the funny goings-on at the opera house. People appeared. Then disappeared. Neighbors said the place was haunted. They said they saw ghosts."

"Ghosts?" Lincoln said.

"Well, have a happy day." She closed the door.

They started on down the street.

Bunky carried his bundle of clothing on top of his head. "I don't believe in ghosts," he said.

"I've never seen one," Lincoln said. He draped the black

cape around his neck so it wouldn't drag on the sidewalk.

Wilbur shifted his bundle from one shoulder to another. "What would you do if you saw one?" he asked.

They all agreed they'd run.

At the drugstore corner they crossed the street and headed for the junkman's.

"How much do you think we'll get for these things?" Wilbur asked.

"Let's go through them first," Lincoln said.

They passed Officer Roberts, busy settling an argument between a couple of drivers.

Lincoln led the way to the front of the firehouse where the sidewalk was very wide. "Let's spread out here," he said.

"We could save the stuff until Halloween," Wilbur said, trying on a celluloid collar.

"That's six months away," Bunky said.

"We could put on a play," Lincoln said.

A shadow fell across the pavement.

Lincoln looked up. It was Officer Roberts.

"What you fellows got there?" he asked.

"Old clothes Mrs. Crauch gave us. We're taking them to the junkman."

"You're impeding traffic. Move on."

They did.

4

THEY WALKED ALONG the side of the red brick firehouse. Where it ended, a high board fence took over. Lincoln peeked through the slats in the gate. An idea popped into his head, like popcorn bursting from a grain. It was followed by another pop and another, until his head felt like it was floating away. "I've got it!"

"Got what?" Wilbur asked.

"A place for our clubhouse."

"Where?" Bunky asked.

"Right here. The firehouse," Lincoln said.

"How you gonna get in?" Wilbur asked.

"I can see the boarded-up door," Lincoln said. "The boards look pretty old. I guess no one's taking care of the place since it's going to be torn down."

"How's it gonna be our clubhouse when it's torn down?" Wilbur asked.

Lincoln grinned. "We'll just borrow it for the initiation. We'll show those Stickballers."

Now Bunky and Wilbur were excited. They boosted Lincoln up over the fence. He fiddled with the rusty lock on the inside of the gate until he got it open. The boys dragged in the clothes and looked around.

"It's about like the back of the drugstore," Wilbur said.

"Yeah, cracked cement and weeds," Bunky said.

Lincoln began to yank at the boards nailed across the door. "Just like I thought. Old," he said.

With the help of Wilbur and Bunky, it didn't take long to get them out of the way. Wilbur pushed in the door, then stood back. "You first," he said to Lincoln.

Lincoln hesitated.

"Scared?" Wilbur asked.

"Who, me?" Lincoln said. Still he felt as if he were wired for electricity as he tiptoed into a large hall. Pale light came through small windows close to the ceiling.

The room was bare but for a brass pole which stood alongside ladderlike stairs which led to a loft.

Lincoln felt strange. He wasn't Lincoln Farnum at all. He was someone who lived years and years ago. His mind saw the red fire engine. The hook and ladder wagon. Stomping horses. Firemen in boots, helmets, and red suspenders.

While Wilbur and Bunky raced around the big hall, Lincoln moved, as if in a trance, and climbed to the loft.

Here the firemen had slept.

Down below, at the far end he saw a raised platform.

The stage? When this place had been an opera house? That's where the actor had disappeared.

"Why?"

"How?"

Lincoln could see no signs at all of the building having once been a railroad station. Mrs. Patch surely got herself mixed up at times.

The building seemed strong. Alive. The floorboards didn't even creak. He'd thought the place would be ready to totter.

The brass pole, even though tarnished, shone in the dim light. He reached over, felt it. He shivered. He felt as if he'd touched the past.

Down below, Wilbur and Bunky were staring up at him.

"I dare you," Wilbur said.

Lincoln reached out again and touched the pole.

He heard bells. Sirens. A call in the night: "FIRE! FIRE!"

A woman and six children were stranded on the fifth floor of an apartment building.

Fireman Lincoln Farnum to the rescue.

Man the pumps; up the ladders.

He swung out on the pole.

"ZOWIE!" he yelled as he shot to the floor.

Wilbur and Bunky raced up the ladder.

Bunky came down slowly. But Wilbur did a flipflop and almost landed on his head.

"I'm going again,' he yelled.

There was a sudden creak—creak—creak——

It came from the direction of the doorway alongside the stage.

Wilbur froze halfway up the ladder.

"The ghost," Bunky whispered.

"It's nothing," Lincoln said, but he felt prickly all over. He walked toward the stage. The others followed close behind. He felt as if he were in slow motion as he climbed the steps.

"CREAK . . . C R E A K . . . C R E A K . . . ."

There it was again. Lincoln felt as if he were in a nightmare. The "Creak" would grab him.

He inched toward the open doorway. He couldn't make his feet walk into the room. He felt like a frozen Popsicle. Stuck to the floor.

Then he saw it. The door of a cabinet moving back and forth. "Creak . . . creak . . . creak."

He doubled up. Pointed. "There's the ghost. . . ."

The three of them laughed at themselves.

It was a large cabinet and went from the floor to the ceiling. It was big enough to walk into. A pole ran across the top of it. "This must be where the actor hung his clothes," Lincoln said.

"I guess he had lots of costumes," Bunky said.

Wilbur and Bunky ran back into the hall, but Lincoln sniffed around. The cabinet had a strange, yet familiar, smell. He looked around the rest of the room. It must have been the actors' dressing room. It was completely bare.

He came out on the stage to find Lincoln and Bunky playing an imaginary game of basketball. Wilbur jumped up high. Made a basket. He dribbled the ball down the court to the other end. Bunky was in hot pursuit.

What a place this would make for a gym.

For lots of things.

Something for everyone on Plum Street.

Why must it be torn down?

"Okay, you guys," Lincoln shouted. "On with our meeting. Now we've got a place. How we going to initiate the Stickballers?"

No one had an idea.

Bunky was trying on the shabby pants, pulling them up to his armpits by the suspenders. "If this is what they wore in the olden days, I'm glad I didn't live then," he said.

The inside of Lincoln's head started to pop again.

"ZOWIE!" he yelled. "GOT IT!"

"Got what?" Wilbur asked.

"An idea for the initiation."

"Well!"

"A TIME MACHINE."

"What's that?"

"A machine to take the Stickballers back over a hundred years in time when this place was an opera house," Lincoln explained.

"You mean you got a machine that can go back to the time people dressed in clothes like Bunky's putting on?"

"We rig up something. Blindfold the Stickballers. Give them a magic potion. Tell them they're going back to the time when this was an opera house and haunted. We scare them like crazy."

Wilbur grinned. "Scaring them like crazy sounds good to me."

"Me too," Bunky chimed in.

Now everyone was excited.

"I'll borrow Uncle Jay's cassette tape recorder. We'll make scary tapes," Lincoln said. "We'll wear these old-time clothes." He picked up the cape and tossed it around his shoulders. Something fell to the floor. A small book. He picked it up. The pages were stuck together. He pried it open.

Wilbur and Bunky came to have a look.

"What is it?" Wilbur asked.

"It looks like an account book. See, it has figures:

'SHIPPED 25 BALES.

ARRIVED GOOD SHAPE.'

Now what comes in bales?"

"Cotton," Bunky said.

"Hay," Wilbur said.

"The actor must have been a farmer, too," Lincoln said. He pried open another page. "Look. Here's a drawing of something. A square box, connected by a straight line to another square box."

Wilbur looked over Lincoln's shoulder. "I'd say it's two trucks on a superhighway ready to crash head-on."

"They didn't have trucks or superhighways that long ago," Lincoln said.

Bunky had a look. "I'd say boxcars on a track."

"No wheels," Lincoln said.

"The guy probably just liked to doodle," Wilbur said.

Lincoln's imagination started popping again. "Maybe it's pointing the way to a secret hiding place."

Now everyone got excited. "Maybe it's a map showing where gangsters hid some loot," Wilbur said.

"No gangsters then," Lincoln said.

Bunky had an idea. "I'll bet pirates hid a chest of Spanish gold somewhere in the building."

Lincoln kind of liked that idea. Maybe if they found something important, it would make the building historical and they could save it. "Where would you hide a chest of Spanish gold, Bunk?" he asked.

"In the loft, maybe," Bunky said.

They raced across the hall, up the ladder to the loft. They tapped panels. Tried to pry open a floorboard. Finally they gave up, slid down the brass pole, and dropped to the floor, exhausted.

Lincoln picked himself up. "We've got just one week to plan the initiation. So let's put it all together."

He was disappointed. He wished they had found something. But he guessed if there was anything about the building that was historical, the firemen would have found it long ago.

5

STILL, ALL THE NEXT WEEK, while they got their props
together and plotted the initiation ceremony, Lincoln kept on
investigating. He found nothing. No secret attic. No hidden
cellar. He even went to the library to see if he could find out
something about old buildings. There wasn't a thing to be
found about the one-time Plum Street opera house.

He bumped into Supervisor Williams in the library. Lincoln was a little in awe of the supervisor, but he went up to
him and asked if there was any chance of saving the
firehouse.

The supervisor shook his head. "It's a closed case," he said sadly.

Lincoln, with Wilbur and Bunky in tow, stopped by to see Mrs. Crauch one day.

"I suppose you want to see the kittens," she said, beckoning them in.

Calico was sitting on a blanket in the trunk, and her kittens were scampering all around.

"You may pick one up," Mrs. Crauch said.

Lincoln picked up the smallest one. He liked the feel of the fur against his face. He listened to it purr. "I guess they like living in the actor's trunk. Can you tell us more about him?"

"Child, that was long, long ago," Mrs. Crauch said. "I didn't know him. My father did."

"Don't you even know his name?"

"Now let's see," Mrs. Crauch said, rubbing her temples with her forefingers. "My father called him 'friend.' So maybe he was Mr. Friend."

That was all Mrs. Crauch could tell him.

"Let's try Mrs. Patch," Lincoln said when they were once again on the street.

"You can't believe anything she says," Wilbur said.

But they walked to the corner apartment, down three steps, and knocked on the door of Mrs. Patch's basement apartment.

She didn't answer until Lincoln had knocked several times. Finally, she opened the door a crack.

"Mrs. Patch," Lincoln began very politely. "We're trying to find out something about the past of the old firehouse. We're wondering why you called it a railroad station."

"Because that's what it was," she said. She began to talk about it, but nothing she said made sense.

"Did you ever ride on the train?" Lincoln asked.

Mrs. Patch covered her mouth with her hand. Her eyes looked scared. "Spies," she croaked. "You're all just spies." She slammed the door shut.

"See, what did I tell you," Wilbur said.

"It's weirdo," Bunky said.

All the way home, words jumbled around Lincoln's mind: railroad station . . . conductor . . . bales . . . ghosts . . . opera house . . . firehouse . . . spies. . . .

6

ALL WAS GOING SMOOTH as chocolate pudding.
It was initiation time.
The props were set up in the hall.
The flashlights were in order.
Wilbur had on the frock coat. He plopped the wide-brimmed black hat on his head. "Who AM I?" he asked.

"I've seen you somewhere," Lincoln said. "But where?"

Bunky hung the high and wide celluloid collar around his skinny neck. His pants ballooned around him.

Lincoln had Uncle Jay's tape recorder cassette fastened under his jacket. He practiced flipping it on and off. With the black cape over his shoulders, the Stickballers would never guess where the scary noises were coming from. And they'd never know that gloomy, spooky voice, was his.

"Okay now," he said. "Let's go over it once more—from the top. First off, when we hear the secret knock, we cover our clothes with sheets."

"Got it," Wilbur said.

"Bunky, you give them the potion," Lincoln said.

"What's in it?" Wilbur asked.

"Water, vinegar, salt, and pepper," Bunky said, rearranging the paper cups on an orange crate.

"Okay," Lincoln said. "Then they go into the time machine. . . ."

There was a rap on the door. A pause. Three more raps. The secret code.

Lincoln felt a shiver scoot around inside him. "Okay. On with the sheets," he said.

The door made a scary squeak as he opened it. It wasn't entirely dark yet. The faces of the Stickballers looked kind of green.

"Jeepers. I didn't know this was your clubhouse," Hands blurted.

"Shush!" Lincoln hissed. "Line up. Everyone who wants to join the Plum Street Athletic Club raise his hand."

All hands went up.

"Who's going first?" Lincoln asked.

Hands swaggered forward.

Wilbur herded the rest of them to the dressing room and stood guard.

Bunky gave Hands a cup of potion.

He took a swallow. Gagged. "Poison. I've been poisoned!" he yelled.

"QUIET!" Lincoln ordered. "Every time you speak out of turn you get a black skull against your name. Three black skulls and you're in trouble."

Wilbur put a blindfold on Hands.

The brass pole was at the other end of the hall, in darkness. Wilbur led Hands toward it, on up the ladder-steps to the loft.

Lincoln flipped on the tape. He listened to his own voice.

It sounded scary all right:

"You are now in phase one of the time machine. You are going back in time over one hundred years to the time when this building was an opera house and I was an actor. Now I am a ghost. In exactly one minute I intend to put you on the time capsule. Grab hold and hang in there, otherwise you will fall to your doom."

Wilbur grabbed Hands, led him to the brass pole. Put his hands around it.

The voice on the tape went on:

"Listen to the count. We are now at ten. . . . thirty. . . . sixty. Blast Off!"

Wilbur shoved Hands' feet off the floor. Hands shot down the brass pole with a whoosh and landed in a heap. "Help! I'm dead," he yelped.

Lincoln flipped on the tape.

Bells rang. Whistles blew.

The "clippity-clop, clippity-clop" of the horses' hooves sounded real, and not at all like the soles of shoes against a floor.

"You are here, in 1862," the tape announced. *"Your friends will soon join you."*

When all the Stickballers had been put through the time machine, with much yelling and squealing, they were led close to the stage and put in a circle.

"Blindfolds off," Wilbur yelled.

The Stickballers looked around.

Lincoln, Wilbur, and Bunky had tossed off the sheets and strutted about the stage in the old-time clothes.

"You're back in the time the firehouse was an opera house." Lincoln announced. "When it was haunted."

"HAW! Haw!" Hands said.

"Haw!" another of the Stickballers echoed, not too loudly.

Lincoln flipped on the tape. Heard his spooky voice:

"I'm the ghost of this old opera house. I'm in pieces. Your job is to put me together again so I may rest in peace." There was a loud moan. *"Oh, where, oh, where is the gravedigger?"* Another loud moan. *"Ah, there he is, beside my coffin."*

"It's Bunky," someone said. "Who's afraid of Bunky?"

"That's about a dozen black skulls you fellows have already," Lincoln reminded.

Bunky flipped a blanket off a box which stood on the edge of the stage.

"It IS a coffin," Hands said.

It was a coffin crate which Lincoln had begged off the local mortuary.

While Lincoln and Bunky, with great ceremony, removed the lid from the crate, Wilbur spread the blanket over the feet and hands of the Stickballers in the circle.

With just one faint flashlight turned on, the scene was eerie. Wilbur gave instructions: "The ghost's pieces must be passed under the blanket, and all around the circle."

Lincoln stuck his hands into the coffin crate and picked up a rubber glove. He had filled it with water, tied it at the wrist, and frozen it in his Mom's refrigerator. It was beginning to leak. He handed it to Wilbur, who passed it, under the blanket, to Hands.

Lincoln turned on the tape. Heard his "cellar" voice:

"Shake my hand, if it makes you shiver,
What will you do when you feel my liver?"

There were shudders and shouts as the Stickballers passed the drippy hand around.

Now Lincoln handed Wilbur a fistful of corn, while the gloomy voice intoned:

"My teeth are loose, but I gotta chew,
If any are missing, I'll sure haunt you."

"Hey, I dropped some, one of the fellows yelled.
Next Lincoln started a soggy sponge going the rounds:

"Here are my brains, don't spill them, please,
Or I'll have you guys down on your knees."

"Hold on to some of them brains," one Stickballer yelled to another. "You could use a few more."

This got everyone to laughing.

Lincoln gave a dried apricot to Wilbur. The "voice" warned:

"This ear was once alongside my head.
Beware! It listens though I'm quite dead."

One of the Stickballers guessed it was an apricot. "I'm gonna take a bite out of that ear," he said.

A bunch of tangled yarn was the next item to make the circle:

"This head of hair is all I've got,
Drop a strand and your bones will rot."

Lincoln had a piece of leather soaking in soapsuds. It sure felt slippery. Wilbur almost dropped it when Lincoln handed it to him.

The tape sounded mournful:

"Now this might feel like an old wet rag,
But it's my tongue, and don't you gag."

When Wilbur handed it to Hands, he yelled and threw it across the circle. It hit one of the Stickballers in the face. He made a wild throw. It smacked Lincoln.

The game broke up.

Everyone started yelling and running around the hall. Hands spotted the brass pole. "So that's the time capsule," he yelled. "Well, I'm for another blast-off."

The rest of the Stickballers followed him up the steps to the loft.

Down they whooshed.

"Everyone back in the circle," Lincoln yelled. "You've all got black skulls against you and the ghost seeks revenge."

"We don't believe in ghosts," Hands cried.

Up the ladder he went again. "I'm coming down one-handed," he shouted.

There was a sudden pounding on the front door. A police whistle. Officer Robert's voice: "Who's there?"

Hands shouted from the loft: "He'll never find us here."

The Stickballers joined him.

"Where were Wilbur and Bunky?" Lincoln wondered.

With all flashlights doused, he couldn't make out a thing.

He heard the back door open, and made for the dressing room. Through a crack in the door he saw the strong beam of the officer's light stream across the hall and up to the loft. "Okay, boys, slide!" He seemed to know exactly where they were hiding.

He'd probably look in the dressing room next. Lincoln tiptoed to the clothes cabinet and got in. He closed the door.

He flattened himself against the back of the cabinet.

It began to move.

It opened out.

He grabbed at the clothes pole to keep from falling backward.

What was this?

His insides quivered.

His skin crawled.

Officer Roberts or no Officer Roberts, he wasn't going to stay in here.

He pushed out of the cabinet and ran.

7

OUTSIDE ALL WAS QUIET.

Then Lincoln heard a whisper. "Link. Over here." It was Bunky.

There was a whistle from the other side of the yard. Wilbur!

They gathered in the darkness. Bunky had some details. Officer Roberts was calling the parents of the boys who were caught. He'd heard him say so.

"We're sure lucky he didn't get us," Wilbur said. "Where were you hiding, Link?"

Lincoln still felt shaken. "In the clothes cupboard. I found something. A secret panel."

"Did you see any Spanish gold?" Bunky asked.

"I didn't see anything. Just a moving panel. Who's for going back in with me?"

Neither volunteered.

Finally, Bunky squeaked. "I will. Tomorrow."

"Yeah, tomorrow," Wilbur said.

Tomorrow sounded better to Lincoln, too. But he was pretty sure this was their only chance. "They'll nail it all up tight again in the morning. I want to know what's behind the moving panel."

"Something that crawls, I'll bet," Wilbur said.

"The ghost," Bunky said.

But Lincoln wanted to find out about the building. Maybe there was something behind the panel that would tell him about the past. He had to know. "I'm going in," he said.

After a moment, Bunky said: "Can't let you go alone."

"I'll never hear the last of it, if I don't go along," Wilbur finally said.

"Okay," Lincoln said. "No flashlights until we get into the cabinet."

They crept to the stage and the actors' dressing room by the pale streetlight coming through the windows. They squeezed into the clothes closet. Lincoln banged the back panel. Nothing happened. He stood with his back against it and pressed hard. The door swung open. He grabbed hold of Wilbur and Bunky to keep from falling backward.

Lincoln flashed his light into the blackness.

"Gosh!" Bunky said.

"Let's get out of here," Wilbur said.

Lincoln flashed his light straight down on the near wall. He saw footholds in it. "There must be something down there," he said.

He was scared. But he was more curious than scared. "I'm going down," he said. "Hold your lights on me."

The hole was about six feet deep. He beamed his flashlight around. "Come on down," he called up. "It's just a cellar."

They climbed down and began to pound the walls. They were of cement. Until they got to the west wall. It looked like the others, but there was a hollow sound. "It's wood," Lincoln said. "Maybe it's a door."

He ran his fingers around it until he felt a crack. "It's stuck shut. Who's got a pocketknife?"

Wilbur did.

"Let's try prying it," Lincoln said.

It was hard work, but they finally got it open a ways.

Beyond was blackness.

And a damp, familiar, smell.

"You gonna go in?" Wilbur asked.

Lincoln had already started.

They followed on behind.

They were in a tunnel. It was maybe five feet wide, Lincoln thought. Shored up.

In the beam of his light, Lincoln saw something way ahead. "Look," he whispered.

"Maybe it's a body," Bunky said.

They approached slowly.

It was a pair of old boots, alongside a bundle on a stick. When Lincoln picked up the bundle, it fell apart. Shreds of old clothing.

They went on. There was nothing more.

"I wonder how far this goes?" Lincoln said. "We must have come a good half block."

Suddenly there was the end. The tunnel was barricaded.

Wilbur tried pulling one of the boards of the barricade. It didn't give. "A tunnel that doesn't go anywhere," he said.

But Lincoln had been thinking. "It goes somewhere, all

right. We came in a straight line from the firehouse. Do you know what I think is on the other side?''

"No, what?'' Bunky asked.

"Our old clubhouse.''

"Gosh, I think you're right,'' Bunky said.

"It's weirdo,'' Wilbur said.

FREIGHTED
TO CANADA...
50 BALES SHIPPED
THIS MONTH
FROM STATION
APRIL 1860
R.R. WORKING WELL.

Lincoln flashed his light around the tunnel. The beam caught something scratched on a wooden support. He aimed the light closer in. Slowly, he made out the writing:

Bales again. Same as in the little book.

"We better go back," Lincoln said. "It's getting late."

His mind was in a whirl. Everything he'd seen and heard was like a jigsaw puzzle that had one part missing. It wasn't possible to complete the picture. He thought about this while they climbed out of the tunnel, went through the cabinet, through the back door of the firehouse—into the waiting arms of Officer Roberts.

"Well, well," Officer Roberts said. "This is quite a catch."

8

LINCOLN WAS NEVER in small trouble. It was always big. This time it was gigantic. He could tell by the number of times the telephone was ringing. Bunky's mother, Wilbur's mother, maybe even Hands'.

It was the morning after the initiation. Lincoln was still in his room, trying to figure how he could sneak out of the house without being seen.

Last night, when Officer Roberts had escorted him home, Pop hadn't come home from his Chicago run. Mom had sent him to his room while she talked with Officer Roberts.

Now Pop was home. Not only that, Uncle Jay and Aunt Charlotte were here for Sunday breakfast.

Well, Lincoln decided, he wouldn't come out. He would stay in his room all day. Starving. Even though Sunday was "French Toast Day." They'd find him, limp. Maybe dead.

He got out the little black book that the actor, Mr. Friend, had written in. But he couldn't put his mind to figuring out what it all meant.

He opened the door a crack. In came a buttery fragrance. The French toast won out. He moved on tiptoes, and slid into his chair.

When he looked up, it was into a ring of frozen faces.

Aunt Charlotte, who had only girls, was always nervous around Lincoln. She fumbled in her purse for her pillbox. "My horoscope today said to expect the worst," she said.

Uncle Jay usually looked at Lincoln as if his face were going to split, but today there wasn't the tiniest crack.

Lincoln didn't even have a chance at one piece of French toast before the doorbell rang. Pop answered. In came Officer Roberts and Supervisor Williams.

Lincoln considered sliding off his chair and creeping under the table.

Mom offered coffee.

Then everyone seemed to fix his eyes on Lincoln.

"All right, Lincoln," Pop said. "Officer Roberts and Mr. Williams are here to find out about last night. They want to know what you were doing in the old firehouse."

"It was Mr. Williams who saw the lights flashing," Officer Roberts said, sipping his coffee. "He called me."

"I keep an eye on the place," Mr. Williams said. "Can't get out of the habit even though it's going to be torn down."

"It shouldn't be," Lincoln said. "It should be used for all kinds of things. The Plum Street Center—"

"Keep to the subject, Lincoln," Pop said.

Lincoln swallowed a couple of times. "Well, we lost our clubhouse and didn't have a place to initiate the new members, so I just thought I'd borrow the firehouse since no one wanted to save it except Mr. Williams. That's all there's to it."

"Not quite," Officer Roberts said. "You hid, and then when I finally caught you, you said you'd been in a tunnel."

"That boy's imagination just keeps on growing," Aunt Charlotte said.

"I *was* in a tunnel. And so were Bunky and Wilbur. I found it because I hid in a clothes closet that moved when I leaned against the back. So after everything quieted down, we decided to investigate."

Mr. Williams stepped forward. "Did you find anything?"

"We found that the tunnel went right under Plum Street, under the drugstore, and ended in a barricade at our old clubhouse."

Aunt Charlotte sighed. "That boy!"

Uncle Jay silenced her with a wave of his hand. "Let Lincoln finish. What was in the tunnel?"

"Just some old boots. Old clothes. Maybe it was part of the railroad Mrs. Patch talked about.

Pop came on fast for Pop. "Now, I'm a railroad man myself. If there'd ever been a railroad on Plum Street, I'd have known about it."

"Everyone knows Mrs. Patch talks nonsense," Sara said.

"She says funny things about today, but she remembers things her father told her," Lincoln said.

Uncle Jay came and stood next to Lincoln. "What else did she say about the railroad?"

"She said it didn't have an engineer, or a fireman, or tracks, or an engine, but it had a conductor. Then when I saw the writing in the tunnel—it was the same as in the book, and it was about freight, so that's when I thought maybe a long time ago there was a railroad that went underground, even if it . . . it . . ."

Lincoln suddenly felt almost paralyzed—like that frozen Popsicle again. And then he was jumping up and down like a yo-yo.

"Underground!" he shouted to Uncle Jay.

"Underground!" he yelled at Pop.

"A real underground." Lincoln's voice dropped to a whisper.

Everyone just watched him.

Except Sassy. "So what's a real underground?" she asked.

Now everybody started talking at once, explaining.

"I read about it once," Lincoln said. "It was how people helped slaves escape to the North and to Canada."

"That's right," Sara said. "Before the Civil War and long afterward. The operation was secret."

"So it was called 'underground,' " Uncle Jay said.

Pop broke in. "The conductor was someone who helped show the way."

"Like Harriet Tubman," Mr. Williams said. "The farms and houses where the runaways were welcome were called 'stations on the underground.' The password was, 'A friend with a friend.' "

"That's what the actor must have been. A 'friend.' Mrs. Crauch called him 'Mr. Friend.' And the costume Wilbur wore last night was what Quakers wore. It belonged to the actor."

"No wonder people thought there were ghosts on Plum Street," Sissy said.

"ZOWIE!" Lincoln shouted. He suddenly had the answer to the drawing. He pulled out the little black book. "Look, this shows the underground. A square box connected by a straight line to another square box."

"I don't get it," Sissy said.

"The first box is the firehouse cellar, then comes the tunnel leading to the second box, which is the cellar under Mr. Woods' drugstore. That's how the slaves escaped."

"Very interesting," Mr. Woods said.

Lincoln was almost afraid to ask. "Does this mean the firehouse is historical?"

"We'll have to *prove* it was an underground station," Mr. Williams said.

Lincoln opened the book to another page. "The actor wrote things in this book that are like the ones I saw in the tunnel. It's a secret language." He read:

Freighted to Canada

March 18 1859 ....
4 large Bales

March 24 1859
2 large Bales
3 Small Bales

"Bales must have been people. The actor was a conductor on the underground. He kept this record—"

Mr. Williams grabbed the book. "Of course, of course," he said. "The 'Friends' who helped the slaves used a secret code. Large bales meant adults; small bales meant children. Sometimes they used the term 'packages' instead."

He flipped on through the book. "This is astounding. I would say that Lincoln has found enough proof to warrant

further study of the firehouse, and to stop the auction of the property at this time."

Then, all of them—Pop, Mr. Williams, Uncle Jay, and the rest talked about financing it. They spoke of things Lincoln didn't understand, like revenue-sharing funds. . . .

"How about charging people to make the 'Freedom Walk' through the tunnel to the coal cellar?" Lincoln said.

"Good idea," Mr. Williams said.

"It's Mr. Woods' property. Would he go along with such a plan?" Sara asked.

"He'd get more business," Lincoln said.

"Well, it looks as if we're going to have a Plum Street Community Center after all," Mom said, smiling at Lincoln.

Pop looked proud.

Even Aunt Charlotte seemed pleased. She gave Lincoln a package of Lifesavers.

The only person not impressed was Baby Herman. He threw his rattle at him.

"Ouch!" Lincoln cried, and ran outside.

He found Wilbur and Bunky on the steps and told them what had happened.

"Great," Wilbur said. "Only thing, where we going to have our club meetings?"

"In the FREEDOM CENTER, of course. How about in the loft? Imagine a clubhouse right under the roof, with a brass pole to slide down. What do you think Hands and the Stickballers will say about the club now?"

"They'll flip," Wilbur said.

"And how!" Bunky said.

"Okay, let's go find them, and start them flipping," Lincoln said.

About the Author

Dale Fife is both an adult and children's book writer. This is her fourth book about the popular Lincoln Farnum. Her other books for children include *Adam's Abc's, Ride the Crooked Wind,* and *Walk a Narrow Bridge,* for which she received the juvenile award of the Martha Kinney Cooper Ohioana Library Association in 1967.

Dale Fife lives in San Mateo, California.

About the Artist

Paul Galdone came to the United States from Hungary at the age of fourteen. After studying at the Art Students League in New York, he began his extremely successful career as a children's book illustrator. He has illustrated more than 100 books and has written and adapted several books for which he also did illustrations. He has twice been runner-up for the Caldecott Award.

He divides his time between his home in Rockland County, New York and his farm in Vermont.